A Spe...

Besides Bijoy Rai ... at the Big Hous... Rajah.

Rajah was st... another man a... ...ting him with—*patterns?* ... ...Prem...terns... red, yellow, pink, black, and white.

"*What* is happening?"

"We are going to the *mela*, Rajah and I," said Bijoy Rai. "We are leading the procession." A *mela* is a fair.

"What *mela?*" asked Prem.

"In Pasanghar."

And, as Prem still looked puzzled, "Don't you know that tomorrow is the beginning of the great *Puja?*" A *Puja* is a holy day.

"Surely," said Bijoy Rai, "you know about Diwali. Why, every child knows about the Festival of Lights."

To his surprise, Prem burst into tears.

Premlata
and the
Festival of Lights

RUMER GODDEN

Illustrated by Ian Andrew

HarperTrophy®
A Division of HarperCollinsPublishers

Harper Trophy® is a registered trademark of
HarperCollins Publishers Inc.

Premlata and the Festival of Lights
Text copyright © 1996 by Rumer Godden
Illustrations copyright © 1996 by Ian Andrew

Library of Congress Cataloging-in-Publication Data
Godden, Rumer, 1907–
   Premlata and the Festival of Lights / Rumer Godden ;
illustrated by Ian Andrew.
      p.   cm.
   Summary: In Bengal, India, Premlata's family is too poor
to celebrate the Festival of Lights until fate and an elephant
step in.
   ISBN 0-06-442091-4
   (1. Divali—Fiction.   2. Elephants—Fiction.   3. India—Fiction.)
I. Andrew, Ian P., 1962–   ill.   II. Title.
PZ7.G54Pr   1999   98-7215
(Fic)—dc21   CIP
                                                                    AC

Typography by Michele N. Tupper
1   2   3   4   5   6   7   8   9   10
❖
First Harper Trophy Edition, 1999

First published in Great Britain in 1996 by Macmillan
Children's Books, a division of Macmillan Publishers Limited.
First published in the United States in 1997 by Greenwillow
Books. It is reprinted here by arrangement with
William Morrow & Company, Inc.

Visit us on the World Wide Web!
http://www.harperchildrens.com

Note:

Before you read this book it is important that you know about Indian money—or some of it. There are little coins, *annas* and *paisas*: *annas* are small and silvery, *paisas* are copper; hardly anyone uses either of them nowadays—they buy so little. People use rupees; a rupee is round and looks like silver—Ravi and Prem thought it was pure silver through and through.

In Bengal, where the story happened, the villagers call a rupee a *taka*.

Chapter 1

"Ma, isn't it time to get out the lights?"

Prem—Premlata—was a little Indian girl living in a part of India called Bengal. She was fair for an Indian child, with big dark eyes and curly hair which always seemed to be in a tangle because Mamoni—Ma—did not have time to comb it. The lights—*deepas*—were tiny earthenware lamps shaped like a leaf and holding a bit of cotton wick in a spoonful of oil. They were for Diwali, the Festival of Lights. On that night, the great Goddess Kali goes out to fight against the demons of evil who spread wickedness, darkness, and bad luck through the world, and all over Bengal people set thousands of little lit *deepas* on courtyard walls, gateposts, roof ridges, along paths and on boats to help Kali in her lone fight. "She hasn't fought for us in years," said Ravi, Prem's older brother.

"Perhaps this year she will." Prem was ever hopeful.

Most children would have been afraid of Kali—she looks so dreadful. The village potter was making a tall image of her for Diwali. So that no one can see her in the darkness, she is black. She has sharp tusks for teeth and her long red tongue is hanging out because she is a tidy Goddess and licks up the blood of the demons she has killed. She wears a necklace of skulls and has four arms so that she can fight better; one of her hands holds a sword, another the head of a giant that she has just cut off—"She can cut off the hugest giant," boasted Prem. She dances in a frenzy, but something in Prem's own fierce little heart loved and trusted the Goddess. "She has to look like that," Mamoni explained, "to frighten the demons and kill them. They are very strong, and remember, she does it to protect us."

In the *puja* or prayer corner of the hut in which they lived, Mamoni kept doll's-house-size clay figures of the gods and goddesses on a bracket. Kali stood out among them, and every night Prem went to sleep sure that her family was safe; no demons would dare to come near them.

"Mamoni, it *is* time to get out the lights."

Mamoni did not answer. She was sitting on the earthen floor sifting rice in her wicker pan, which was shaped like a dustpan. She was so skillful that the good rice grains went to one side—not a grain must be lost—while the husks flew out onto the ground. It would be Prem's task to sweep them up with her small grass broom; though Prem was only seven, she had to work hard.

Mamoni had been beautiful but now, like Prem, she was too thin; her cotton sari was worn thin, too. As she worked, her bangle slid up and down her arm and, watching, Prem seemed to remember that once Mamoni had had many bangles, gold and silver ones. This one was cheap bronze and its metal had gone dull, but Mamoni would not have parted with it for all the world: "It was the first present Bapi, your daddy, gave to me when we were boy and girl." All the rest of her jewelry had gone, as so much had gone since Bapi died. Prem, though, still had her little silver nose-ring that he had given her when she was a year old. She wore it in one nostril, which had been pierced to hold it. She did not remember the piercing, only how pretty she looked with the ring. It was sad that there could be no nose-ring for Meetu, her toddler sister, but Meetu, who had been born after Bapi died, was so roly-poly and happy she would not mind. It was Ravi and Prem who minded.

"Mamoni, everyone in the village has brought out their lights."

The village was Prem's world—she could hardly remember the town of Pasanghar, three miles away, where they had lived with Bapi. The village was on a knoll above a pattern of paddy fields; paddy—rice—is grown in water and the water glinted in the sun; white paddy birds waded across it. Small clay tracks led between the fields, paths just wide enough to take a bicycle, a rickshaw, or a careful elephant.

The village itself had coconut palms; more narrow little lanes led between the houses, most of them huts with earthen walls and floors, thatched roofs, and earthen-walled courtyards. There was a smell of hot dust, smoke, and mustard oil from the cooking fires.

In the center of the village was a wide tank or pool where, in the early morning, the villagers washed their clothes and themselves, dipping a *lota*, a small brass pot, in the water and pouring it over their heads and bodies as they said their morning prayers, always facing the sun. Beside the pool was a sacred banyan tree, where the village men sat in the evening, and by it a temple, its pointed roof made of hammered-out kerosene tins that looked like silver. The villagers thought it handsome. The priest who looked after it was another of Prem's friends.

On all sides of the village stretched the great plain. Except for a few other knoll villages, it was so flat that the sky seemed like a great bowl turned upside down to meet the land all around.

There was, too, the Big House of whitewashed brick. It belonged to Zamindar Bijoy Rai. *Zamindar* means landlord, and he owned most of the villages and the land.

"We lived in a brick house, too, when we were in Pasanghar," Ravi often told Prem, "and don't you forget it." Prem could not forget it because she could not remember that time—only in glimpses like Mamoni's gold and silver bangles.

Bijoy Rai had let Mamoni have the hut. It had only one room, where she and Prem slept on the only bed, made of wooden planks. Meetu could still just fit into her cradle, while Ravi slept on a camp bed outside where the roof thatch came down to make a little veranda; their night quilts were kept tidily rolled up against a wall. There was a *chula*—a small clay cooking stove—a low shelf for a few brass cooking pans, a *lota*, and small earthenware bowls for drinking tea. They all ate sitting on the floor, using banana leaves for plates. They had one big tin trunk, painted with roses, where Mamoni kept their clothes and a few treasures she had saved; a hand-lantern hung on a hook, where it did not give much light, and most important, there was the *puja* corner.

Every morning, Mamoni put marigolds there—she grew them in the courtyard—

and made an offering, a few grains of rice and a piece of fruit for Kali and the others.

"It *must* be time to get out the lights," said Prem.

Again Mamoni did not answer.

There had been great excitement in the village because Bijoy Rai's house had just got electricity. In his kindness he had run a line to the banyan tree—there was even talk of a radio—and already there was a big floodlight on a post. "That should help the Goddess," said Prem, but the electric light was so still and glaring that she liked the little flickering *deepas* better; each tiny flame looked alive as if it, too, was fighting the darkness. "Mamoni, please, please, get out the lights."

This time Mamoni did speak. "I can't," she said. "We have no *deepas*."

"But we *have*."

"Not now."

"But . . . "

"I had to sell them," said Mamoni.

"*Sell* them!" Prem knew that Mamoni had sold not only her jewelry but her better saris, almost all their pots and pans, their paraffin lamp . . . but the *deepas!* "They are for the *Goddess*," Prem wanted to cry. Tomorrow night in the lit-up village theirs would be the only house in darkness, the only house not to help Kali, the only house left to the demons.

"Mamoni." Prem said it in a small pleading voice. "You can't. We can't . . . "

"*Premlata!*" Mamoni did not often say "Premlata" like that, but when she did Prem knew it was no use arguing any more, especially when Mamoni went on, in her everyday voice, "Now, I want you to take these pots of curd and these cheeses to the Big House and tell Paru Didi I want the muslins back." Mamoni would wash them and use them over and over again to protect the pots and cheeses. Prem flinched: Paru Didi, housekeeper at the Big House, was not good at giving things back. "The pots of curd are seven rupees each, the cheeses fifteen, so Paru Didi must give you fifty-one rupees." Mamoni sighed: that was less than half the price they would be in the shops. "Fifty-one, don't forget. Don't drop the basket. Go straight there and back and don't daydream."

That was more easily said than done: Prem loved going to the Big House. Behind the veranda with its arches, the rooms were spacious and cool after the hut. They were built around an inner courtyard with a purple-flowered jacaranda tree, roses, a red hibiscus, and a tap. It was a marvel to Prem that anyone should have a tap of their own: there was only one for the whole of her village.

An outside staircase led up to a flat roof with a parapet. Bijoy Rai slept and spent most of his days up there so that Prem seldom saw him, though she would have liked to. Her father, Bapi, had been his trusted clerk, looking after land, villages,

money, everything, while Bijoy Rai sat on his daybed in the shade of a roof umbrella, entertaining visitors, smoking a hookah, drinking tea or sherbet, eating sweets and fruit.

He was a fat, jolly man. Both he and Paru Didi were fat: "All that good eating!" the villagers said wistfully. Even for every-day he was always dressed in a *dhoti*—loincloth—of fine white muslin folded and fanned out in front and, with it, a long tunic shirt without a collar made of silk, a heavy gold necklace, and rings set with jewels that the astrologers—holy men who believed in the power of the stars—had told Bijoy Rai were lucky for him. His shoes were hand-made with a hooked-up toe, and he finished his toilet with a touch of scent. He also wore horn-rimmed spectacles that made the villagers respect him even more: few people in the village had spectacles.

Bijoy Rai's wife had died and he had no children of his own, but seemed to like them. Once he had invited Prem up on the roof; he let her sit on his daybed beside him and talk—he seemed to know how to make children talk—and had given her a slice of papaya, that luscious golden fruit with black seeds, and let her help herself to *gaja*, sugar puffs. In the kite-flying season he let the village boys come up to fly their kites from the roof's height and seemed to enjoy the kite battles as much as they did. The kites were made of paper and light bamboo; their strings had been dipped in ground glass and glue which made them as sharp as a razor. Each boy crossed his kite string with another boy's and they battled, moving and lifting their string rollers until one kite was cut loose. It was exciting. "You should go up with the other boys," Prem told Ravi.

"*Boka!* Silly!" Ravi said. "How could I ask Mamoni for two rupees to get a kite? And don't I have to look after Dhala?"

Dhala was their beloved water buffalo.

She was called Dhala, meaning "fair," because although she was dark gray she had a small white spot on her forehead. Dhala was big enough for Ravi to ride on her back; she had long curved-back horns, her nose was soft and broad, while her eyes were dark and kind and had lovely long lashes. She lived in a lean-to shanty at the back of the hut and was part of the family. Through all their troubles Mamoni had kept Dhala. "Kept!" said Mamoni. "She keeps us."

Dhala gave them milk, enough for all of them and for Mamoni to make the curd and soft cheese she sold to Paru Didi. Sometimes a farmer would hire Dhala to plow or to pull a cart, but Mamoni was careful of that: a driver could be cruel and twist a buffalo's tail or let the heavy wooden yoke rub her neck raw. Dhala even gave them her dung: if she dropped any while she grazed, Ravi would gather it up carefully in a basket and bring it home, where Mamoni would take a lump and plaster it on the hut's outside wall, pressing it flat with her open hand so that each pat had her finger-prints. When the dung had dried it made good slow-burning fuel for the stove.

Every day, all day, Ravi took Dhala to graze on the plain. How else could they have fed her? Because she was a water buffalo, he had to take her first to the field water hole, where she sank with only her nose showing and the tip of her horns, which was buffalo bliss. In the evening he brought her home—"cow-dust time," the villagers called it, because the cattle, treading the clay paths, raised the dust. Then she had to be milked, and given a pail of water and some hay and husks for the night.

Ravi was ten, a dark, handsome boy, but he was angry and bitter—because it seemed that nobody cared. "I should be at school," he said to Prem—never to Mamoni.

Prem knew he did not mean the village school but the big one at Pasanghar, where he had been top boy of his class. "I would

walk the three miles there and back if only I could go." How much nicer, Prem thought, not to go to school, sitting, chanting lessons, having drill, being ordered about, instead to be out on the plain with Dhala, dreaming under a blue sky, but, "I need to be at school," mourned Ravi. "Soon I'll forget how to read."

There had been a day when, coming home early, he had met Mamoni going out. She was carrying their hand-lantern and tried to hide it in her sari, so that Ravi knew at once she was taking it to sell to the moneylender. "You can't do that," he had said.

"Son, I have to. We have the little oil lamp . . . " But Ravi had taken the lantern and put it back on its hook.

"*I* am going to the moneylender," he said. "I am the man of the house now," and he had gone to the shelf where he kept his books, the few that had been saved.

"No! No!" Mamoni cried. "You can't do

that. You'll need these books some day."

"What day?" Ravi had asked in scorn. "We need the lantern *now*." He tied the precious books into a bundle and went out.

Now he really might forget how to read, and at supper that evening Prem put out a hand to pat him. He shrugged her off. "Stop that! I'm just a buffalo boy, I tell you." But later that night she had found him in Dhala's stall, his face pressed against the big hairy neck, and he was weeping. She had gone away on tiptoe.

Ravi's books, and now the *deepas*. Prem was too shocked to cry.

"Wipe your feet," Paru Didi ordered before Prem had come into the Big House kitchen. "I don't want your dust on my clean floor." Prem could not leave her shoes outside, as is the Indian custom, for she had no shoes, and, true, her feet had been dusty, but she had wiped them as Mamoni always made her and Ravi do.

Didi means "elder sister" and Paru Didi was elder sister to all the villagers but, like some elder sisters, she was forever scolding them and telling them what to do. She was a big woman and heavy; her saris were starched—Mamoni starched them—so that they rustled importantly as she moved. She wore more jewelry than Prem had ever imagined on anyone: heavy gold earrings, a nose-ring, toe-rings, bangles, necklaces. Her small black eyes were sharp: they saw every fault and now, taking up a pot as Prem put her basket on the table— Paru Didi did not work on the floor as most women did, since the Big House had tables and chairs—she said almost at once, "This curd is not properly set."

Prem felt her lips grow tight. She knew she must not be rude, but she said, "Mamoni makes the best curd."

"No one asked your opinion, young miss. Well, for your mother's sake I'll take it, but that will be twenty rupees off."

"Mamoni said fifty-one rupees." Prem suddenly became brave, though she had to dig her nails into her palms.

"Fifty-one rupees when the curd is so poor!" Paru Didi's voice was shrill. "Well, say thirty-two. Take them and go."

Prem, like Ravi, could be angry. She thought of Mamoni toiling over her cooking and dared to say, "Fifty-one or I'll take them back," and she began to put the pots back in the basket.

"You are talking to *me?*" Paru Didi seemed to swell.

"Yes. We can sell them to the sweetshop *easily.*"

Paru Didi was flummoxed. She knew that was true, and nowhere could she buy curds and cheese as cheaply as from Mamoni. "Forty," she said, and counted out forty coins on to the table.

"Fifty-one." Prem held on to the basket.

Furious, Paru Didi put down the extra eleven and swept the coins onto the floor.

As Prem knelt to pick them up, Paru Didi bent, held Prem down with a heavy hand on her shoulder and, with the other hand, gave her a hard slap on the cheek—so hard that the kitchen seemed to swim around Prem. Before she knew what she was doing, she had turned her head and bitten Paru Didi's hand.

She heard Paru Didi shriek but, clutching all the rupees, Prem seized the empty basket and ran.

Outside she had to stop. Her legs were trembling, her breath came in gasps; her cheek burned and stung. She knew Ravi would be proud of her—but Mamoni? She would be horrified—and afraid. *I can't go home yet,* thought Prem. *If I saw Mamoni I would cry.* Small girl though she was, Prem was not going to let Paru Didi make her cry.

She was standing beside the staircase that led to the roof and she had a longing to go up and see Bijoy Rai, but Mamoni had said, "You must never worry Zamindar

Babu." She had a deep respect for Bijoy Rai and called him Babu, or sir.

Prem gave a little sob, then, like a wise child, she decided she would go and see Rajah.

Besides Bijoy Rai, Prem had another friend at the Big House: Bijoy Rai's elephant, Rajah, who was almost as dear to her as Dhala. Rajah lived in the high elephant stable and had a courtyard of his own; Bijoy Rai used him for going over his land and visiting villages and was proud of him. All elephants are big, but Rajah was huge; Rajah means "king" and he was a kingly elephant, as gentle as he was big.

Prem loved him and he seemed to love her, even though she came only halfway up his leg; he had great ivory tusks, big flapping ears, little eyes that saw everything, and a long trunk. When he saw Prem, he always salaamed as his mahout, Naleen, had taught him, putting the tip of his trunk to his forehead. A mahout is the man who looks after an elephant and drives him, sitting on his neck. Prem always salaamed back and always, on her way to see him, picked Rajah a tuft of grass, which he accepted as politely as if it were a whole stem of bananas, taking it with the end of his trunk, which was pink, and putting it in his mouth, which was pink, too.

Prem picked a tuft of grass now but, as she came to the elephant courtyard, what was happening?

Rajah was standing with Naleen and another man on either side of him on ladders, and they were painting him with—*patterns?* thought Prem—patterns in red, yellow, pink, black, and white. Naleen was painting Rajah's forehead with a lattice of red and yellow; all down his trunk the pattern went, with white dots. The other man was doing his sides, and the elephant's toenails were already painted scarlet.

Suddenly Rajah was impatient—perhaps he had seen Prem with her tuft of grass. He

flapped his ears. The second man fell off his ladder as, "*Aré! Shaitan!* You devil!" cried Naleen, which was no way to speak to a rajah.

In the courtyard, too, was Rajah's howdah, the padded wooden seat he wore on his back when he took Bijoy Rai around the village. It was like a four-poster bed without legs and had a small, pointed roof. Two of Bijoy Rai's gardeners were dressing it with a red velvet cover for the seat and roof, and they were winding gold cords around the posts with tassels that ended each in a bell.

Four anklets of red leather with little tinkling bells lay beside the howdah. When it was time, they would be tied around Rajah's legs. Prem could imagine the lovely sound they would all make with every one of Rajah's giant strides.

"Why? What?" cried Prem.

Naleen did not answer. Bijoy Rai was there, sitting on an upturned empty oil drum, watching every brushstroke.

"*What* is happening?"

"We are going to the *mela*, Rajah and I," said Bijoy Rai. "We are leading the procession." A *mela* is a fair.

"What *mela?*" asked Prem.

"In Pasanghar. It's a big *mela*, with swings and carousels, storytellers, conjurers, stalls of lovely things," and, as Prem still looked puzzled, "Don't you know that tomorrow is the beginning of the great *Puja?*" A *Puja* is a holy day, and in Bengal the people worship Prem's own warrior goddess, Kali. "Surely," said Bijoy Rai, "you know about Diwali. Why, every child knows about the Festival of Lights."

To his surprise, Prem burst into tears.

Bijoy Rai could not bear to see anyone cry, particularly a little girl. He drew Prem against his knees as he sat on the drum. "There, there!" he said. *"Ki holo! Ki holo!* What has happened? Tell Bijoy Rai. Tell." And Prem told.

For a few moments Bijoy Rai was silent,

only patting her with a large, comforting hand. Then, "Sold your *deepas?*" and she thought she heard him say, as if he were talking to himself, "Is it as bad as that?"

Prem nodded.

Bijoy Rai gave a great sigh. "Every home should be lit. It is for our Goddess," and he felt in the pocket of the waistcoat he wore over his tunic, bringing out a fat purse. Before Prem's astonished eyes he counted out thirty-five rupees. Thirty-five! Prem counted every one with him. He had, too, a little cotton moneybag; now he put the rupees into it, pulled the string tight, and gave it to Prem—it was quite heavy. "Tell Srimati Devi"—Mamoni's real name—"to go to the potter and buy new *deepas.*" But, almost as he said it, another plan came into Prem's head. It had begun with what he had told her about the *mela*, which had enchanted her: swings, carousels, story-tellers, conjurers, stalls full of lovely things! And it was a daring plan: she would go to the *mela* and buy the *deepas* herself.

But how?

On her way home Prem began to see how.

Tomorrow, Mamoni was to be at the Big House from early till late, helping Paru Didi make dishes and sweets for the *Puja*—Bijoy Rai would have many visitors, and there would be fireworks in the evening. Prem knew she would have to look after Meetu all day. Mamoni would leave them their midday food: a bowl of cooked rice, milk to soften it, and molasses—brown sugar syrup.

Prem would take it and Meetu to Shanti, her best friend; Shanti and her mother were fond of Meetu and liked looking after her. "I have to work," Prem would tell them—after all, buying the *deepas* was important work. They would think she was at the Big House and she knew they would never be bold enough to go there. "I'll bring you a pretty sweetmeat," she would promise Shanti, guessing that Mamoni would manage to bring home a few from the Big House for the children.

That fitted in nicely but—and here Prem stopped. The *mela* was in Pasanghar and that was far away. Ravi said three miles. Some of the villagers would be going, but they were grown-ups and certainly any grown-up would tell Mamoni. Prem guessed the bigger boys would go, perhaps all together in an oxcart, but she had better not beg a lift from them: they would tease her and might steal her bag of rupees. At cow-dust time, when Ravi brought Dhala home and had milked her, Prem asked him, "Dada"—older brother—"are you going to the *mela* with the other boys?"

She knew he could not and, sure enough, "*Pagli!* Are you crazy? Don't I have to look after Dhala?"

"You"—Prem nearly said "We"—"you could ride there and back on Dhala."

For a moment Ravi's eyes lit up, and she

knew how much he would have liked to go to the *mela*, then they clouded. "And when would she feed? We can't buy food for her." So Ravi was no good. *I shall have to walk,* thought Prem. But how long would that take her? *I shall have to. . . .* Then, suddenly, she thought of the postmen.

Every morning, one came from Pasanghar on his bicycle, bringing the mail which, in their village, was mostly for Bijoy Rai. As he liked his letters and parcels early, the postman on duty would come riding on his way home through the village no later than nine o'clock, long after Mamoni had gone to the Big House and Ravi had taken Dhala to graze. That would give Prem plenty of time to carry Meetu to Shanti and get herself ready.

Then she would stand by the path that led past their hut to the main road to Pasanghar, and stop the postman. She hoped it would be the young one, Arun, who was quite a friend: Mamoni often gave him a drink of

coconut milk and he would laugh with her
and Prem. Above all, he would not ask
grown-up kinds of questions. "Please," Prem
whispered to the Goddess Kali, "please let
it be Arun."

If only I had something to wear. Prem had
come back from Shanti's, where Meetu
seemed perfectly happy, and was getting
herself ready. She had grown out of
the pretty clothes she used to have in
Pasanghar—Mamoni was keeping them
carefully for Meetu—and she had only two
frocks, one being washed, the other worn,
and they were old, gray not white. She did
not wear anything underneath. There was
nothing else until suddenly she remembered there *was* something else . . . but
dare she? Almost fearfully, as if someone
were looking, she went over to the tin trunk,
opened it, searched, and found, wrapped
in thin paper, what she was looking for: a
child-size sari and bodice that Mamoni had

worn as a little girl. She had kept them for Prem; there had never yet been a time when she could wear them, but now . . .

The sari was pink muslin with a pattern of tiny gold flowers and a border of gold, the bodice gold-colored to match. Prem knew how to put the sari on: one end around her, knotted at the waist, the long end, gathered up in pleats and tucked in—the pleats were not as good as Mamoni's—while the other end of the sari went around her back and over her right shoulder, its end hanging loose. She washed her face and hands, combed her hair, hung the precious bag of rupees around her neck, hiding it under the sari, then went into the courtyard, picked a *champa* flower to put behind her ear, and waited.

The small walled courtyard was a peaceful place; rush mats were spread on the ground and the family often sat there. There was a grass broom, and *gamalas*, big earthenware pots, stood in the shade;

Mamoni filled them with water every morning from the village tap, carrying them balanced on her hip. Flower creepers grew over the walls, pumpkin vines with yellow flowers, and, best of all, there was the *champa* tree with waxen-petaled flowers smelling so sweetly that the air was filled with their scent. At dusk, Mamoni would come out to light a lamp at the foot of the sacred little *tulsi* plant on its platform of clay and blow a conch, a big shell, *ullalu-ullalu,* a peaceful sound to welcome the evening and say good-bye to the day. Now it was morning and Prem was ready, waiting for the swish of the bicycle: "Please, *please*, let it be Arun."

It was Arun: she heard his whistling coming nearer, no one whistled like Arun, and went on to the path in case he should fly past—he always rode fast. "Arun, stop! Stop!"

The dust flew up as he braked. "*Aré dushtu!* Naughty! I nearly ran over you."

"Arun, would you—could you take me to the *mela*?"

Arun did not say, "My! You look fine!" as Prem had hoped he would; he had finished his round and only wanted to get back to the *mela* himself. His bicycle had a small back carrier on which he set his mailbag. The bag was empty now, so he took it off and hung it on the handlebars. "Hop on."

Prem would not have believed they could whiz through the paddy fields so fast, leaving a trail of dust. The paddy birds flew up, men working a water mill shouted, then they were on the main road and went faster, past oxcarts bringing villagers and the boys, who shouted, too, and waved. Prem could not wave back—she had to hold tightly to Arun's postman's coat while the end of her sari flew up like a flag.

"Tarra-rarra-tarra," sang Arun.

"Tarra-rarra-ra," sang Prem.

"Look through the spectacles of love, everything is good," Arun sang.

"Everything is good," Prem echoed.

> *Light, chase the dark away,*
> *no more fighting and bickering,*
> *crying, moaning.*
> *Hug me and smile.*

Prem would have liked to hug Arun, but her arms were too short.

"Tarra-rarra-tarra."

"Will you see the procession?" Prem asked when the song was over.

"I might; will you?"

"I must," Prem said proudly. "I have a friend in it. Rajah. He knows me."

"A rajah knows *you?* That's likely!"

"He does. Rajah is an elephant," said Prem, but now they were getting closer to Pasanghar, and Arun had to dodge around little three-wheeled black-and-yellow taxis, which blasted their horns at him. He went faster than the laden bicycle rickshaws that Prem could not remember seeing before—

they could not go down the village's narrow paths. She thought them pretty with their hoods patterned in blue or pink stuck with gold paper flowers and stars in honor of the *Puja*. Then there were streets and houses, Pasanghar itself, and Arun stopped at a large open space loud with noise and crowded with tents, stalls, a throng of people, while far above them, in the air, a big wheel turned, all sparkling in the morning sun, as the bicycle stopped.

"Hop off," said Arun.

Chapter 2

Arun had not waited, and for a few minutes Prem could not move or even think. There was too much noise, too many people jostling around tents and stalls, children running in and out shrieking; goats, dogs, taxi horns, a band playing, loudspeakers blaring, music blaring, too, from different tents, with streamers, pennants, flags. There were jugglers—she could see their balls flying up in the air—and storytellers with a crowd around them. Peddlers carried long poles top-heavy with toys, and fans made of palm leaves or peacock feathers. Some stood on boxes shouting the things they had to sell.

When she looked at the children, the sari and bodice, of which she had been so proud, seemed suddenly old-fashioned. The little girls wore party dresses with many flounces and gathers, while the boys had brightly colored jackets, and she thought miserably of Ravi's old thin vests and shorts. Soon, though, excitement began to tingle in her, too, right down to her toes. "But I have to buy the *deepas* and find Rajah," she told herself, and pushed into the crowd. No one took any notice of a little girl until she asked a woman, "Where is the procession?"

"The procession? That's not till the afternoon."

The afternoon! Prem had meant to see the procession, buy the *deepas,* and go straight home but, *Oh, well!* she thought, *I'll buy the* deepas *first and wait.* It was then, though, that she saw the swings. On one side of the *mela* was the fun-fair. She could make nothing of the giant wheel up in the sky, or the coconut shies, or the big carousels high above her head, but there was a line of swings and suddenly she remembered how, long, long ago in Bapi's day, she and Ravi had had a swing in a garden where Ravi pushed her. Now the thrill of going backwards and forwards higher and higher seemed to come back. "*Kee sundoor!* How lovely!" She could not help herself: she joined the queue and, sliding her hand under her sari so that nobody would notice, she found the bag and took out her first rupee. "Two rupees," said the man, and reluctantly Prem took out another, but she felt Ravi would have encouraged her.

It was as wonderful as she had thought and she did not want to get off, but she had to find a potter and buy the *deepas*, "first," she told herself firmly, but beside the swings there was a carousel, not big like the others but small-girl size. The mounts were swans, tigers, camels, and ponies, one of them a little white pony, hooves red, its glossy flanks painted with flowers, its mane and tail flowing. "*Kee sundoor!*" all of Prem seemed to breathe. She slid her hand in to find the bag and took out another two rupees. Next minute she was on the pony, holding its scarlet reins, and music began to play.

Prem had never, of course, ridden on Rajah, although she had dreamed of doing that; she had ridden on Dhala, but Dhala was lumbering and slow; she had been on Arun's bicycle, but his bicycle did not go up and down. Nothing was like the little pony: "*Kee sundoor! Kee sundoor!*" She held on tightly to the reins and his mane while his red hooves seemed to prance as he moved up and down and the music tinkled. The wind blew in her hair; it was pure joy, and when it stopped she could not get off but took out still another two rupees and, when the second ride was ended, would have

taken out two more, but other children were waiting and she had to get down. As she gave the pony a last pat, a bigger girl pushed her aside; it was a hard push that seemed to say, "The *deepas!* The *deepas!*" Then, "You *must* find out where Rajah is, you silly girl," she scolded herself.

Opposite the fun-fair was a long line of stalls selling . . . *everything,* thought Prem: cooking pots and pans, cloth—she could see baby jackets in bright colors hanging up—*how Meetu would have loved one of those*, but Prem knew they were expensive. Saris were draped on stands—*Mamoni needs a new sari.* Thinking of Mamoni, there were jewelry shops with piles of colored-glass bangles, red, green, black. There were grain stalls, stalls selling sweetmeats, kite stalls bright with paper kites. *There must be a potter somewhere,* thought Prem, but before she reached the end of the stalls, a peddler stood in her way. From his pole he took a paper windmill on a stick, its little pink-and-blue sails spinning around in the breeze. "Take, *baba*," he said. "For you."

Not for me, thought Prem at once, *for Meetu*—Meetu had never had a toy. But the windmill, it seemed, was not a present: "One rupee," said the peddler.

It was only one rupee but, "The *deepas*," Prem reminded herself. "I must buy them first." Yet she seemed to see Meetu's eyes shining, her gurgle of delight, and turning her back to the peddler so that he could not see the moneybag, she took out the rupee.

Holding the windmill carefully, Prem was going slowly along the stalls looking for a potter when she smelled a tantalizing smell, hot cooking oil, and with it a sound of sizzling. She was standing by a cookshop and the cook was frying samosas, savory puffs of crisp batter stuffed with potato and spices, nearly ready to eat. "*Kee bhalo!* How scrumptious!" Prem felt almost faint: she had not known how hungry she was. She had left Mamoni's rice, milk, and molasses for Meetu, and had had nothing since early morning. "You must eat," Mamoni was always telling them, and, "I still have plenty of rupees," Prem argued with herself.

Surprised at her own boldness, she went to the shop.

The cook was polite and, as soon as Prem asked, he took a sizzling samosa and put it on a banana leaf for her. "Let it cool," he advised, but the moment it had cooled a little, she gobbled. Like most Indian children, Prem ate nicely with her hands. When she had licked the last crumb off her fingers, she could not resist another.

Then the man began to hand out small cones filled with something white, creamy and cold.

"What is it?" she asked.

"*Kulfi*," he said, which is Indian ice cream. Prem had never even seen it—*kulfi* did not come into the villages. "Try," he added, giving her a cone, and before she could stop herself she had taken a lick. That was enough. She had never tasted anything like it.

"*Kee bhalo!*" and, "Could I—could I have one more?"

She had two more.

"*Sandesh?*" asked the shopkeeper, showing the sweets, little squares of cream cheese melted with sugar and topped with silver paper.

"*Kee bhalo!*" But Prem remembered her promise to Shanti: "I'll bring you a sweet-meat."

"Only one rupee," the shopkeeper was tempting her, but sense stirred in Prem.

"How much does it all come to?" she asked.

"With *sandesh?*"

"Just one," she made herself say, and was glad she had, because it was a shock when he said the bill was eight rupees, ten *annas*. "You must find the *deepas* at once," she told herself, "look for Rajah, see the procession, and go *home*," but Prem was not used to having her small stomach full, more than full with three *kulfis*—at home they got up from their meals still hungry— and the sun was high in the sky now and hot. She was suddenly so sleepy she could hardly stand after all, she had started early, getting Meetu ready, herself dressed, waiting for Arun, the bicycle ride, "Tarra-rarra-ra," the excitement of the *mela*, the swing, her little horse. She gave a huge yawn.

By the wicker wall of one of the stalls was a wooden plank bed. It was in the shade and empty. She looked around fearfully, but no one was near it and she lay down, putting the windmill carefully beside her, keeping her sari over the bag, which was still comfortably heavy. In a moment she was fast asleep.

When Prem woke, she sat up rubbing her eyes because they were dazzled. It was late afternoon and the *mela's* lights had come on: lights along the lanes between the stalls, which themselves were lit; lights flooding the grounds; strings of colored lights on tents, which were bright inside. Some of the crowd carried hand-lanterns; the lucky children had torches which they flashed. The *mela* was even more beautiful and exciting but, *I must have slept too long,* she thought in panic and then, "The procession! Rajah!" she cried, springing from the bed.

She must have cried it aloud because a big boy jeered, "*Gadha!* Donkey! The procession is over."

"Over!"

"Yes, long ago."

Prem's heart gave a sickening thump. "It can't be."

"It is."

"Then I won't see Rajah." Rajah in all his lovely patterns. "I won't see Rajah!" It was bitter and, as she stood there, another sickening thump came: she had forgotten Meetu's windmill. *I must have left it on the bed!* She tried to run, but there were too many people. When she reached the bed the windmill was gone.

Poor little Meetu! How disappointed she would be. It did not come into Prem's mind that Meetu could not be disappointed—she knew nothing about the windmill. "I must get her another." She could not see the peddler, but perhaps there was a toy stall. She went along the stalls and there was indeed a toy stall—and such a toy stall!

It had a whole rack of windmills, pink-blue, pink-green, green-yellow, yellow-red, and how she, Prem, would have loved a basket of tiny brass pots and pans, or a cut-out wooden man who moved his arms and legs on strings. She yearned after a toy horse: white, like her carousel pony, it was even painted with flowers. "No," she told herself, "you have had the swing and the carousel, the lovely food. Meetu has had nothing," and on that came another thought: Ravi had had nothing—and Mamoni.

With the thought of Mamoni, a wave of homesickness came over Prem. She felt she had been away from Mamoni far too long, and she seemed to see her as yesterday when she had so patiently sifted the rice, the worn, old bangle sliding up and down her thin arm. Then, once again, Prem seemed to see further, to those long ago golden and silver bangles that had been on Mamoni's wrists when they lived with Bapi and, "I'll buy her a silver bangle *now*," vowed Prem. She knew gold would be too expensive. She forgot everything else and took a windmill—she had come back to pink and blue. The shopman charged her a rupee more than the peddler, but she could not stop to argue, and pushed her way back through the crowd to where she had passed the bangle stall.

She did not like the look of the bangle-stall seller. He was fat and oily, sitting cross-legged wearing a silk tunic and small round embroidered hat. Sure enough, "*Jao*. Go," he said. "I don't give baksheesh to children."

"I don't want baksheesh." Prem felt angry that he had thought she was begging for money. "I want a silver bangle."

"Silver! Don't waste my time."

"Real silver," said Prem.

Perhaps he had taken in her sari, because he spoke more gently: "Silver's not for children."

"It's not for me. It's for my Mamoni."

"Take her a glass one, baba."

"Silver."

He began to laugh. When he laughed his stomach shook, and, "I'm not laughing," Prem said in disgust. "Silver—or I'll go to another stall."

"*Nah, nah*—No," and "Ah!" he said. "I believe I have the very thing—somewhere." He turned the heaps of bangles over. "The very thing," and from under a pile he drew out a silver bangle. Prem caught her breath. It looked so perfect. Although it was not all silver, it had pinhead-size

studs that caught the light.

"What are those, winking?"

"Diamonds," said the man, with his oily smile.

Prem did not know what diamonds were, except that they were prettier than anything she had seen, but she had to be sure. "Is the bangle real silver?"

"Do you think I would sell you a bangle that wasn't?" He twirled it around. "Doesn't it shine?"

"Yes! Oh, yes!" Prem thought she would die if she could not get it for Mamoni. "How much?" she asked, trembling.

"For you—ten rupees."

"Nine," said Prem—something made her say it and, to her surprise, he nodded. How kind! She did not see that his stomach was shaking again. He even found her a little box and put the bangle in with a piece of pink paper. Prem was so radiant as she turned away that she did not notice how much lighter the moneybag was now.

* * *

Prem had the bangle and the windmill: she could imagine Mamoni's and Meetu's delight and she was delighted, too—but what about Ravi? Why should Ravi be the only one left out? She knew how dearly he would have liked to come to the *mela*—and didn't he have to look after Dhala, day in, day out, as well as help Mamoni run the house? Ravi must have a present, too.

A present . . . but what? There were kite shops, but kites were of no use to Ravi; another stall had shoulder bags and purses, but Ravi had no possessions, no money to put in them. It was then that she saw a stall of a kind new to her—there was not one even in the streets of Pasanghar. This stall was filled with books of all sizes, all colors, laid out on trestle tables. *I'll buy Ravi a book*—she nearly cried it aloud. Of course. Then he won't forget how to read.

A young man was starting to put away

the books. "The stall is open?" Prem was anxious.

He shook his head. "I'm going home."

He was not like the other stall-keepers: he was young, dressed in a spotless flowing white tunic-shirt and white pajamas—loose white trousers. He was thin, dark—*and unhappy*, thought Prem at once, *unhappy like Ravi.* "No one buys books at a *mela.*"

"I do," said Prem.

"*You* do?" He put the books down. "A picture book?"

She shook her head. "A book with lots of reading. It's for my brother, Ravi. He's old. He's ten. He was top boy when he went to school."

"Ah!" and Prem found she was telling this young man about Ravi and everything; how Bapi had died, how Mamoni had to sell their things one by one, how Ravi, his own self, had sold his precious books to help and was now just what he said he was, a buffalo boy. "He says he'll forget how to read," said Prem with tears in her eyes.

"*Nah, nah.* Phew!" The young man gave a low whistle. "He must not forget."

"He won't if I buy him a book."

"I know." He went to a tray, picked up a book and opened it in front of Prem. "I used to love this book when I was ten. It isn't new, but it's a good copy." It looked perfectly new to Prem, bound in blue, stamped with gold. It had bright pictures and she gazed at them as if her eyes could rake out their meanings. "It's about heroes and adventures, and look," said the young man, "it has questions; he could write down the answers."

"If he had a pencil," said Prem. Ravi's pencils had been worn down, all his paper used up long ago; he had tried to write in the dust of the courtyard with a pointed stick, but the dust blew away, the stick broke, and he had thrown it away in disgust. "He'll need pencils and paper," said Prem.

"Ah!" The young man went to another tray and came back with a writing book. Prem had never seen a writing book like it: its red cotton cloth covers were stitched in white and it had strings to tie it, "because it's a secret book," he said. "Ravi can write in it anything he likes, not only exercises, and no one can look."

Prem knew that would suit Ravi exactly but, "How much?" she had to ask.

"Could you pay four rupees for the book? I can let you have the writing book for two." Prem could guess it must really cost more than that. "Is that too much?" he asked.

Nothing, Prem thought, could be too much for such beautiful books, especially when he laid two pencils on top of them, "The pencils are from me," so she took out her moneybag—she knew with certainty she need not hide it from him—and counted out six rupees. Again, she was too excited to notice the limpness of the moneybag. The young man found her a string mesh bag to put everything in—including the box with the bangle and the windmill. "I think you should go home now," he said. "Tell Ravi he's luckier than I am. I haven't a little sister like you."

Prem would have loved to stay longer with him—she had not really looked at books before—but he was already putting up all his shutters. It was getting late, too, and she knew she had to go. She went as far as the next corner and stopped. What did she see? A potter!

He was painting a tall figure of the Goddess Kali, shining black, the silver sword shining in one of her hands while painted red blood dripped from the giant's head in the other. She was enough to frighten anybody and Prem gave a gasp, but it was not because of Kali: at her dancing feet were two large baskets of *deepas*.

The string bag had fallen—*thud*—to the ground. *Deepas*. She had completely forgotten the *deepas*. *How could I? How could I?*

That's what I came for. Aré Aré! she felt like wailing. Frantically she pulled out the money-bag. It chinked, which was heartening, but her fingers trembled as she opened the string. Inside were no rupees, only six *annas*.

Six *annas!* Even Mamoni, she knew, could not buy much with that. It was still money, though, and *deepas* were cheap. She went timidly into the shop.

The potter was too busy to hear her. He was painting the Goddess's fierce eyebrows with a fine brush.

"Please," Prem said loudly.

"What is it?" His brush did not stop. He was not kindly like their own potter.

"How many *deepas* for six *annas?*"

"One," said the potter.

If the sky had fallen on Prem she could not have been more crushed.

"You mean," she found her voice, "six *annas* each?"

"*Hain.* Yes," said the potter.

Prem did not cry: she was too desolate.

She was seeing one little *deepa* burning forlornly on their gatepost while every other hut and house was sparkling with lights.

"Please," she begged the potter, "please, you have so many. *Please.*"

"*Jao, baba.* Go away, child. Go."

For a moment Prem could not go, she was so angry with herself. How could she have been so silly? She should have bought the *deepas* and gone straight back home. *That's what I came for!* Then why? But she knew quite well why—knew too late. They would have no *deepas*—she could not bring herself to buy just one, it might as well be none—and on top of that came another hurt: she had not even seen Rajah. She had spoiled the whole day.

As she remembered Rajah, she remembered Bijoy Rai. What would Bijoy Rai say? She had not done what he told her, and she quailed. Prem, though, was a sensible little girl, good at cheering herself up. It was not all spoiled: she had the string bag full of wonderful presents: Meetu's windmill, the book and writing things for Ravi, and, above all, Mamoni's silver bangle—just looking at that would help.

She took out the box and there it was, shining and winking. Diamonds. They sounded rich until, with a sad little chill, Prem remembered what Ravi had always told her: "If anyone ever gives you a rupee, bite it to see if it's real. Silver should be cold and hard." Prem bit the bangle. It was not hard but smooth and faintly warm. It was plastic. Not real silver, plastic!

Now she really did cry, with tears that seemed to burn. The crowds, the lights, the whole *mela* seemed to be laughing at her, as had the nasty, fat stall-keeper when he cheated her over the bangle. She smarted when she thought of it, but what could she do, a child against grown-ups? No one came and asked what was the matter. What was one little girl in such a crowd? Mamoni, Ravi, Bijoy Rai were far away, there was no one. *Only myself,* thought Prem and, when her sobs had died down, Prem said to Prem, "You must go home."

It was then she realized that although she had planned so carefully how to get to the *mela* with Arun, she had not given a thought as to how she would get home. *Oh! I need a grown-up.* There were plenty in the crowd, but none for her. She thought of going to look for one of the village oxcarts, but she knew there would be questions and the boys would snatch the string bag from her. She thought of the kindly young man in the book stall, but he had gone. Then she knew there was only one way to get home: walk. "I can't." Already she was tired out, her legs were aching, her bare feet sore. "How can I?" The answer was, "You must."

Daylight was fading: Ravi would be bringing Dhala home, Meetu asleep, Mamoni cooking. When she thought of Mamoni, Prem gave a little gulp, picked up the bag, and walked.

Chapter 3

Prem walked and walked and walked—she felt it must have been for miles, yet she had only just come out of the town and the road stretched before her into the far, far distance. It was built high above the paddy fields: in the waning light she could see water glimmering in them. And it was strangely empty. All the traffic had gone. There were only a few trees along it, yet endless telegraph poles. She tried to count the poles: *If I can get from one to the next, I won't notice the distance as much.*

Then something else glimmered—a

glimmer that moved. A snake was gliding across the road, leaving a track in the dust. Prem stood stock-still. She knew about snakes, but what kind of snake was this? Too big for a krait, that deadly little snake; it could be a cobra. Ravi would have got a stick but, usually, if you let snakes alone, they let you—unless you trod on them. "I might have stepped on it," she said to herself and, as the snake went quietly over the side of the road, "When it's dark I might tread on another," but she had to go on. Now she could not see the poles: darkness comes quickly in India—one minute it is cow-dust time, the next minute, night. There were no lights, no moon—there never *is* a moon at Diwali time—only starlight shining faintly so that she could just make out the road. It was the silence that frightened her. Not a sound, as if the night was waiting. Waiting for what? And it was so lonely: the villagers were in their villages unless they were staying on at the *mela*. Prem's feet

began to drag, the bag seemed to grow heavier and heavier; it was as if she were walking in her sleep.

A big bird flapped across the road, startling her awake. It gave a screech, "Auk! Auk!" which sounded horridly across the fields. For a while she walked more quickly, flagged again, and froze: by the side of the road two big, shining, yellow eyes were looking at her. She knew they were animal eyes and that they were watching her.

Could they be a jackal's? Do jackals eat children? She had heard them howling at night around the village, but jackals hunt in packs and there was only one pair of eyes. Then she remembered a tale Ravi had told of a leopard that had been seen on the plain. "Leopards spring on you and maul you," Ravi had said. To go on down the road, Prem would have to pass it. Her hands were damp, she could feel trickles of fright-sweat running down her neck. "Somebody! Somebody come!" but there was nobody. Kali! If only Kali would come out of the sky, with her four arms and her sword. "Kali, Goddess, help me," whispered Prem. Kali would not be afraid of ten leopards. "Kali, *please*," but maybe Kali was angry because she, Prem, had not bought the *deepas*. Nobody came.

Perhaps if I keep quite still, she thought, *it will go away,* but the eyes seemed to be coming nearer.

Prem never knew what would have happened, because in the silence she heard a faint tinkling of bells that grew louder and with them a heavy tread, tread. The eyes vanished as the road was lit up by two flaming torches set each side of a howdah, high up above her. The howdah was red, and down the road, in his trappings, tassels, and colors, came Rajah, back from the *mela* with Naleen on his neck. In the howdah sat Zamindar Bijoy Rai.

Bijoy Rai was in party clothes. His tunic was brocade woven with silver thread that caught the light, as did the jeweled clasp in his turban. He wore necklaces and rings. He might have been a prince.

Standing in the road, Prem was so small that Naleen did not see her. Bijoy Rai was too high, but Rajah stopped at once. "*Aré! Dushtu!* Naughty!" shouted Naleen, prodding him, but Rajah would not budge. Instead he made the salaam he always gave Prem and, without being told, knelt down.

Next moment, Naleen had swung down, picked Prem up, handed her to Bijoy Rai, and she was safe in the howdah.

"*Premlata!*" Bijoy Rai could not have been more astonished. "What in the world are you doing here? But you're shivering." He wrapped her in his own warm shawl, holding her close. Her eyes were still wide with fear. "There, there," crooned Bijoy Rai. "*Ki holo, ki holo,*" as he had yesterday in the court-yard. "It's all right. Nothing can hurt you." Then, as he saw the precious string bag she was clutching, the windmill peeping out of it, "You've been to the *mela* all on your own!"

"Yes." It was a whisper.

"To buy the *deepas* instead of letting your Mamoni?"

"Yes. No." She struggled out of the shawl to sit upright. "Zamindar Babu. I didn't buy any *deepas*."

"But I gave you thirty-five rupees."

"I know. I *know!*" Tears flooded again.

Without any more questions, he gathered her back into the shawl and its warmth and said, "Tell." To Rajah's reassuring steady tread, tread, tread, Prem told.

When she came to the part about leaving Meetu with Shanti and waiting for Arun, Bijoy Rai said, "You would make a good army general for planning," and then she told him how, in the *mela*, with the swings and carousel, the stalls, the rupees seemed to fly out of the bag.

"I spent them all until there were only six *annas* left."

"Exactly what I should have done myself," said Bijoy Rai.

"But I'm sorry. So sorry," she sobbed.

"Show me these wonderful presents."

Prem showed the windmill ("Meetu's never had a toy"), Mamoni's bangle ("It isn't real silver like the bangles she had to sell"). Prem could not help another sob. "The man said the little stones are diamonds." She sounded uncertain.

"They'll be diamonds to Mamoni," said Bijoy Rai.

When they came to Ravi's books and pencils, Prem smiled and said, "Now he won't forget how to read."

Bijoy Rai asked, "Why should he forget how to read? Surely he goes to school."

"He can't. He has to look after Dhala."

"Dhala?"

"Our water buffalo. Now he's only a buffalo boy. He sold his books for Mamoni."

"Is it as bad as that?" Bijoy Rai said, as he had said in the courtyard, and again seemed to be talking to himself. "May the gods forgive me! I am a fat, lazy man!"

"No, no." Prem could not bear that. "Zamindar Babu, we love you."

He did not answer. Instead he patted her and said, "Better keep these presents secret till tomorrow. It's good to give presents at Diwali."

Diwali! All Prem's unhappiness and shame came flooding back. No *deepas!* No *deepas!* But before she could begin to cry again, they were at the gates of the Big House.

Bijoy Rai told Naleen to stop, while he gave orders to the gateman. "Go quickly to Srimati Devi's house and tell her I have Prem *baba* safe and well. As soon as she has had some tea I will bring her home," and, "Order a rickshaw."

"I would take you on Rajah," he told Prem, "but he has had a long day and must have his supper."

Rajah knelt at the house steps while

Naleen lifted Prem down and set her on the veranda. She stood blinking at the brilliant electric light as Paru Didi, who had seen them getting off the elephant, came rustling out. "You've got Premlata," cried Paru Didi, but Bijoy Rai did not hear her—he was giving Rajah some pieces of sugarcane. "You naughty, naughty girl! Your Mamoni's been frantic. The whole village is out searching for you. Look at you! What a sight!"

Prem was indeed a pitiful sight: the sari was draggled and brown with dust, her hair tousled—the *champa* flower had dropped off long ago; her face was tearstained and, again, she was shivering. "Where have you been?" Paru Didi was shaking her. "Where have you been? Answer me. Answer at once."

"Paru Didi, not now." Bijoy Rai had said good night to Rajah. "She's exhausted. Go and make her some tea with hot milk and plenty of sugar."

"Make tea for a naughty child? Zamindar Babu, you don't know how naughty she is— and so cheeky. I've had to slap her."

"*Slap* someone else's child?"

"Certainly. Only yesterday."

"Paru Didi, *tea!*"

When Bijoy Rai spoke like that even Paru Didi had to obey, but after she had gone he asked Prem, "Why did Paru Didi slap you?"

"Because I wouldn't take thirty-two rupees for the curd and cheese Mamoni had made for you."

"How much curd and cheese?"

"Three pots and two cheeses."

"Thirty-two rupees for three pots of curd, two cheeses! This is robbery!"

"That's what I thought."

"What did you do when Paru Didi slapped you?"

"Bit her," Prem had to say, but instead of Bijoy Rai looking shocked, she thought she heard him chuckle.

There was a rush of footsteps as some-one hurtled in from the garden and up the veranda steps. It was Ravi. "Prem! Prem's with you! Oh!" She had thought he would scold; instead he was hugging her, kissing her; his eyes were red as if he had been crying, too. "We thought you were lost, kid-napped. Zamindar Babu, thank you, thank you a million times for bringing her home."

"I didn't bring her. She brought herself until fortunately Rajah saw her."

"Rajah!" Paru Didi, who had been listening from the kitchen, came rustling back with a tray of steaming metal tea glasses for both children, a china cup and saucer for Bijoy Rai. She banged down the tray on the veranda table and was going to speak when, "Thank you, Paru Didi," said Bijoy Rai. "That will be all. You may go," and she had to go.

The tea was hot and sweet. "You have some, too," Bijoy Rai said to Ravi. "You look almost as tired as Prem."

"Zamindar Babu, I should take her home. My mother . . . "

"A rickshaw is coming. You'll be there more quickly than you could walk—in any case, Prem's too tired and, Ravi, while you drink your tea you can tell me a few things that I heard from her and I don't understand. Why did your Mamoni have to sell her jewelry and the *deepas?* Why did you sell your books?"

"For money," said Ravi.

"But I paid Srimati Devi every week for working here and helping Paru Didi."

"Oh, no!" said Prem—the tea was beginning to revive her. "That was to pay for our house. Paru Didi said so."

"What?"

"Excuse me, Zamindar Babu." Ravi was being very polite and grown-up. "Did you give the money directly to our mother or to Paru Didi to pay her?"

Bijoy Rai looked at them both and gave a low whistle. "I see," he said. "I see."

Paru Didi was back again. She was curious to know what they were talking about and had found an excuse to come out: she was holding something quite heavy in a basket. "What do you want?" Bijoy Rai said sharply.

"Zamindar Babu, tomorrow is the *Puja*, Diwali. There is much to be done. The house must be ready, so I am clearing out the old rubbish."

"What rubbish?"

"We have electrics now," she boasted to the children, "strings of electric bulbs, all colors, so we have no use for these old things. We have so many of them. I'll put them on the dustheap."

"What old things?"

"Deepas."

"Deepas!" There was a shriek—a shriek of joy—as Paru Didi tilted the basket, which was full of the little lamps, each with a matching wick. Prem was across the veranda. "Paru Didi, don't put them on the dustheap. Don't! Don't! Give them to me,

Paru Didi, please, *please!"*

"Get out of my way."

"Give them to her. They mean nothing to you." Bijoy Rai interfered, but Paru Didi held on to the basket.

"I give nothing to naughty girls."

Then Prem spoke. She, who had been so tired, was standing up straight, her eyes shining. She seemed to have grown since the morning and Bijoy Rai and Ravi watched in amazement as she spoke. "Paru Didi, they are not for me. They are for the great Goddess Kali. I think she sent them. Give me the basket *at once,"* and Paru Didi gave it.

Then, because this one last effort was all she could do, Prem sank to the floor.

She knew nothing about going home in the rickshaw with Ravi, nor that Mamoni, without a word but with tears of joy, had put her to bed, taking off the sari and bodice without waking her, nor that she slept until the middle of the morning, Mamoni keeping the villagers out. They were agog to hear everything Prem could tell. And when she did wake . . .

There was never such a Diwali!

Prem had to tell about the *mela* over and over again, first to Mamoni and Ravi when she gave them their presents. Meetu sat entranced, watching her windmill turn; Mamoni had more tears in her eyes when she saw the bangle. "To me they are diamonds," she said, just as Bijoy Rai had said she would. As for Ravi, he was struck dumb when he saw his book of adventures, the secret writing book, the pencils. When he did speak, he said, in his Ravi way, "*Pagli!* Crazy! No wonder you spent too much money!" Then, "I'll never sell these—I'll keep them forever and ever and ever."

After that the whole village came and heard Prem, even the village priest, who blessed her. "Great Kali protected you and brought you safely home." Some, particularly the women, called her naughty, the men said she was "doughty," which means "brave," and all were agreed that the animal on the road was a leopard. "Certainly a leopard with eyes as big as that!"

In the afternoon, she and Mamoni set out the *deepas*, on the gateposts, along the courtyard walls, over the door and window, around the *tulsi* plant. There were so many that they gave some to Shanti with the *sandesh* sweetmeat Prem had promised. Shanti was overcome when she saw the silver paper: "I'm never, never going to eat it."

"You will," said Prem.

When the *deepas* were all set out, "It's so beautiful," she said. "Kali will be pleased."

Then Ravi had a surprise for her. He had told only Mamoni, but now Prem had to know, too. Before the rickshaw had left the Big House, Bijoy Rai had said, "Tell your mother I would very much like all of you to come with me on Rajah to see the lights, and to stay to watch the fireworks. I will come for you on Rajah at dusk. Ask her to be ready."

They were ready. Mamoni had managed to wash and dry the little sari and bodice; she combed Prem's hair and put a fresh *champa* flower behind her ear. She had been to the courtyard to put the little lamp in front of the *tulsi* plant and sound the conch— *ullalu-ullalu*. She had found a little jacket for Meetu that had belonged to Prem; Meetu would not be parted from her windmill, so it had to go, too. Long ago, Mamoni had made a shirt for Ravi from a silk one that had been Bapi's. For herself she had only one of her cotton saris but it, too, was clean. She wore the bangle, and the diamonds winked beautifully.

Ravi had made a garland of marigolds for Dhala—she had *deepas* in her stall. "I wish you were coming, too." They had just lit the last of the *deepas* when they heard bells:

there was Rajah—still in all his finery—and there, sitting in the howdah, was Bijoy Rai.

It was a magical night, so magical that none of them talked—Rajah's swaying had sent Meetu to sleep. They rode majestically, high above the huts, all with tiny flickering flames; little rafts of lights and flowers had been floated on the village tank and were reflected in the water, the temple roof was outlined so that its silver shone. They went through the fields, where *deepas* were set along the narrow pathways that glittered with their lights and, high above, the bowl of the sky, dark now, was full of stars that did not flicker but were still. *Surely, with so much light, Goddess Kali would win*, thought Prem. Then back to the Big House, where Paru Didi's gaudy electric bulbs, red, blue, green, seemed too bright for magic, but the magic was not over yet.

They had expected to go back to the hut. Instead, Bijoy Rai took them to the Big

House, where Naleen told Rajah to kneel down, then helped them off. "Before the village comes for the fireworks," said Bijoy Rai, "we'll have a Diwali feast."

Ravi and Prem clapped, Meetu woke up, but as Bijoy Rai led the way to the dining room, Mamoni held back. "Won't Paru Didi mind?"

"Paru Didi has gone."

"Gone!" They stared at him in astonishment.

"You've sent her away?" asked Ravi in glee.

"Indeed I have."

"Poor Paru Didi," said Mamoni.

"She wasn't poor. On the contrary, she had been making herself rich for years. Srimati"—he used Mamoni's first name—"she didn't only cheat you, she cheated me. I should have seen it, but I'm such a lazy man. She bought things at half price—the people were too afraid of her to bargain—then she charged me the full. Isn't that cheating? I had believed she was paying you, Srimati, for your work in this house: I gave her the money for your work every week."

"And she kept it!" Ravi was still shocked.

Prem was shocked, too, although she did not say anything. Mysteriously she felt a pang of pity for Paru Didi. The Diwali supper was delicious, and some of the things the children had never tasted: *loochi*—crisp fried bread; potato curry; *payesh*—rice pudding; sweet fruits; and, at the end, *rasa golla*—balls of cream cheese coated with glossy golden syrup. There was lemonade and Coca-Cola to drink. "That was a feast," said Mamoni when they had finished and she was wiping Meetu's face and hands. "A real feast!"

"You ought to know," said Bijoy Rai. "You cooked most of it. Srimati Devi, I have been wondering if you would like to go on cooking for me, and housekeeping. I should be very, very much obliged if you would."

Mamoni almost covered her face with the end of her sari, as Indian women do when they are shy. *"Neesh! Choi . . . "* she whispered, which means "Indeed, yes, but . . . "

"But . . . "

"Zamindar Babu, the children . . . "

"I have no children of my own," said Bijoy Rai, "but their Bapi was like a son to me, a good son, and I should like to be good to his son and little girls. I should have taken better care of you all long ago, and I could if you moved into the Big House with them and we all lived here."

"Kee sundoor! Wonderful!" Prem could not help saying.

"Ravi must go back to his school."

"He can't," said Prem. "He has to look after Dhala."

"My buffalo man will do that and take great care of her. Ravi will have a bicycle for going to Pasanghar."

"A bicycle!" Ravi's breath was taken away.

"I'm sure he'll be top boy again and you, little miss, will go to school, too."

"Not me," said Prem in alarm. "I have to look after Meetu."

"Mamoni and I will do that," but, seeing her lip tremble, "If you go to school you can help Naleen look after Rajah," and, before the last firework star had fallen, ruby red from the last rocket, it was settled.

"Mamoni," whispered Prem, when Mamoni bent over their bed to say good night to her—their last night in the hut; they were to move next day—"Mamoni, can we take her with us?" She pointed to the little figure of Kali shining black in the *puja* corner.

"Of course. We can't do without her."

"And we'll keep Diwali for her?"

"Every year."

"But . . ." For a moment Prem struggled up in bed in alarm. "Not with Paru Didi's electrics."

"With *deepas*," promised Mamoni.